First published in hardback in Great Britain by
HarperCollins Publishers Ltd in 1993
10 9 8 7 6 5 4 3 2
First published in Picture Lions in 1994
1 0 9 8 7 6 5 4 3

Picture Lions is an imprint of the Children's Division,
part of HarperCollins Publishers Limited,
77-85 Fulham Palace Road,
Hammersmith, London W6 8JB

ISBN: 0 00 193820-7 (Hardback)
ISBN: 0 00 664376-0 (Picture Lions)

Copyright © Nick Butterworth 1993
The author asserts the moral right to
be identified as the author of the work.

Printed and bound in Singapore.

The Rescue Party

NICK BUTTERWORTH

Collins

An Imprint of HarperCollinsPublishers

"What a perfect day for doing nothing," said Percy the park-keeper.

Percy was having a day off.

He and some of his animal friends had brought a picnic to one of their favourite places in the park.

Percy took off his cap and made himself a sun hat by tying knots in the corners of his handkerchief. Then he propped himself against an old tree stump and opened his book.

The animals settled themselves around Percy and waited for tea.

It was warm in the sunshine and soon
everyone began to doze. Suddenly they
were disturbed by the sound of laughter.
Percy looked up. Three young rabbits,
two brothers and their little sister,
were playing a leaping game
in the long grass.
When they saw Percy,
the rabbits waved.

"Hello Percy! We're pretending to be hares."
Percy chuckled and waved back as the rabbits went leaping away.

The three rabbits were having a
wonderful time.

"I can jump the longest!" said one.

"I can run the fastest!" said his brother.

"I can jump the highest!" said the smallest
rabbit and she jumped high into the air.

"Wheeeee!"

B ut as the little rabbit landed, to her brothers' surprise, she completely disappeared!

She had crashed right through the rotten cover of an old well.

The two brothers stared at the hole in the ground. Then they began to wail.

"Help! The ground has eaten our sister!"

"Help! Somebody help!"

Somebody, of course, meant Percy.

The two rabbits ran straight to him and told him what had happened.

The other animals looked worried as Percy listened and sighed.

"There's no water in that well," he said, "but it's very deep." He pulled on his cap and jumped to his feet.

"We'll need a rope," he said. "Come on."

P ercy raced away with the animals
following behind him.

Before long he was leading them back
again towards the old well. Over his
shoulder, Percy carried a long rope.

Percy cleared away the rotten wood that had covered the well, and peered into the dark hole.

He couldn't see the little rabbit. She was perched on a log that had wedged itself half way down the well.

"Helloooo," called Percy.
"Can you hear me?"
A rather cross little voice answered.
"I bumped my head."
"But are you alright?" asked Percy.
"I bumped my head," answered the cross voice again.
"Hmm," said Percy, "I think she's alright."
"We're sending down a rope," called Percy.
"Tie it nice and tight and we'll pull you up."
Percy lowered the rope into the well.
The little rabbit wasn't quite sure what to do, so she tied it tightly to the log that she was sitting on.
"Now, heave-ho!" said Percy.

Percy pulled on the rope, but nothing
happened. He pulled again.

"What's she been eating?" he muttered.
"She weighs a ton." He pulled once more,
but still nothing happened. Percy frowned.

"Alright," he said, "let's see what we can
do together."

own in the well, the little rabbit
was beginning to get used to the
darkness. As she gazed around, she noticed
that there was a small opening in the wall
of the well.

"I wonder where that leads to," she said.

At the top of the well, the rescuers lined up behind Percy, ready to pull on the rope.

"Ready," shouted Percy. "Heave!"

Something in the well moved.

"Keep going," said Percy, "she's coming."

The rescuers pulled and pulled. They grunted and groaned and quacked and squeaked.

Up came the rope. But as it reached the top, the rescuers got a terrible surprise.

There was no little rabbit on the end of the rope. All they had pulled up from the well was a great big log!

"Well I'm blessed!" said Percy. "What's happened to her?"

ercy and the animals began to laugh.
They laughed and laughed until they
couldn't stand up.

"But how did you manage to get out?"
asked Percy at last.

"It was easy," she said. "I found a secret
passage. It comes out just over there."

"Well I never!" said Percy. "Well, well, well.
Which reminds me," he added, "I must
make a new cover for that old well."

"I'll do it tomorrow," said Percy as he
led the way back towards their picnic.
"After all," he said, "today is my day off."